Vrell Sparrow

JILL WILLIAMSON

NOVEL TEEN PRESS

Also by Jill Williamson

FICTION

Blood of Kings Beginnings

Vrell Sparrow

The Blood of Kings Trilogy

By Darkness Hid

To Darkness Fled

From Darkness Won

Blood of Kings: Legends (2025)

Squire of Truth

Lord of Winter

Lady of Shadows

Heir of Light

The Kinsman Chronicles

King's Folly

King's Blood

King's War

The Safe Lands Trilogy

Captives

Outcasts

Rebels

The Thirst Duology

Thirst

Hunger

Magic Hunters

The Journey Begins

The Rising Rebellion

The Final Battle

The Mission League Series

The New Recruit

Chokepoint

Project Gemini
Ambushed
Broken Trust
The Profile Match

Stand-Alone Titles
Replication

Non-Fiction

Storyworld First: Creating a Unique Fantasy World for Your Novel
Go Teen Writers: Write Your Novel
Go Teen Writers: Edit Your Novel
Punctuation 101: A Fiction Writer's Guide to Getting it Right

Preface

When I set out to write this little story, I was certain I had never mentioned when Vrell last saw Prince Gidon. Only after I had finished did I stumble upon a couple places that now offer contradiction. First, in *By Darkness Hid*, Vrell mentions that the prince had threatened to send guards to provoke a favorable answer to his proposal, which was why she went into hiding. Second, when Vrell watched Achan fight the poroo to keep "Prince Gidon" safe in the forest outside Mahanaim, there Vrell thinks about the last time she saw Prince Gidon at a tournament in Nesos.

Rats! These two little sentences destroyed all of my fun!

But then I decided I didn't much care. I mean, Obi-Wan Kenobi said in *The Empire Strikes Back* that Luke must go to Dagobah and see Yoda, the Jedi master who trained him. Yet in the prequels, we discover that Qui-Gon Jin was the one who trained Obi-Wan. Such is the way of prequels.

So, I decided to publish *Vrell Sparrow* despite these discrepancies. Yes, I realize that Vrell had that thought about the tournament in Nesos. If I could edit that line in *By Darkness Hid*, I would instead have it say, "The last time Vrell saw the prince, he was standing in her mother's private dining room, trying to force her to marry him."

Alas, since I cannot, I ask those of you who have read *By Darkness Hid* to suspend disbelief and pretend with me. Vrell *was* standing in the Evenwall, after all, when that thought crossed her mind about seeing Prince Gidon in Nesos. And one can never be certain of the surety of one's thoughts in such a place, so near Darkness. As Sir Gavin once told Achan, "A man can go crazy in the haze and never find his way out." So, while Vrell did not go crazy in the Evenwall that day, the magical place *did* cause her to blank out this entire story. Isn't that strange?

Thanks for imagining with me.

~Jill

To my patrons on Patreon.com.
Thanks for reading this first draft
and for your continual support.

1

Rarely did frigid temperatures excite Lady Averella Amal, but when Master Pytel chose the pre-dawn hours of the morrow for harvesting the ice wine grapes, Averella was not about to miss it.

She awoke at the appropriate time and bade her maid, Syrah, help her dress. Along with her warmest twill-weave gown, she donned woolen stockings, an insulated petticoat, her fur-lined boots, and her winter bonnet.

"Are you sure you'll be safe without Master Rennan?" Syrah asked as she helped Averella pull on a pair of mittens over her kid gloves.

Averella bristled at the question. "I have joined the harvest many times before Bran ever started accompanying me."

"Yes, but never in the middle of the night, my lady," Syrah said. "At least not since your father passed."

Four years ago. For pity sake. "Syrah, I am a grown woman and the heir to Carm Duchy. No one would dare bother me with so many

1

witnesses present. Nor would any villain be lurking in the fields on a night like this."

Three hours later, however, Averella's bravado and excitement had long since faded. Her fingers had gone numb beneath her gloves and mittens, and she was no longer certain even the best ice wine was worth the trial of harvesting grapes in the dead of a moonless night with nothing but flickering torches and distant warming barrels to light the way.

Despite her fatigue, Averella kept pace with the workers. Gently cradling a cluster of grapes in one hand to avoid bruising, she fumbled to grip the shoot with her other hand. Thankfully, when she twisted her fingers, the brittle stem snapped free. Averella dropped the heavy cluster into her basket—which was nearly full—and reached for the next one.

In years past, Bran Rennan had worked alongside her and had taken breaks to rub warmth into her hands. She missed his presence, not only here on this cold, dark night, but seeing him each day. His warm smile and easy laugh brought so much joy to her life. Surely it would not be long before she could call him her betrothed.

Mother had all but accepted his proposal and simply needed to find the best way to announce that the heir to Carm Duchy was going to wed someone from a lesser family, which would undoubtedly annoy certain members of the nobility.

Bran would call such people *stodgy*. Averella grinned, which made her cheeks feel evermore stiff in the cold. She reached for the next cluster of grapes and found she could see her movements better than before. A glance at the horizon showed the pale light of dawn approaching. The sight pulled forth a deep sigh of relief which fogged the air before her face. They were nearly finished.

What must it be like for those who lived in Darkness on the western side of Er'Rets? To never see the coming dawn? After ten years of the curse, Averella supposed people had grown used to it. Nothing grew in Darkness, so they had no need of harvesting, but surely there was still much outdoor work to be done. Carpentry and masonry and tanning and hunting... shepherding, too, though Averella could not imagine what the livestock in Darkness grazed upon.

A shout pulled her gaze down the row where a horse and cart approached. As it drew near, workers converged upon it, dumping their baskets. Good. Averella needed more space too.

By the time the cart reached her and she emptied her basket onto the glistening pile of frozen grapes clusters, the twilight morning enabled her to see the harvest somewhat clearly. She liked the look of the grapes. Large. Nice color.

This was a good year.

No crop was as tricky to harvest as ice wine. It could only be made in certain regions and then only when the weather was just right. A bone-chilling frost brought about the best results. Some winters it never got cold enough. Thankfully, this year had experienced extremely miserable temperatures, and Averella was glad some good would come from it. Carmine needed to remain strong and economically stable.

This would be a tumultuous year for Er'Rets, what with Prince Gidon coming of age. He would undoubtedly petition the Council of Seven for the right to rule as king. Mother did not believe he had the votes. Many, Mother included, preferred his uncle, Prince Oren, for the crown. The Council of Seven had been governing Er'Rets until the Crown Prince came of age, but in the past two years, the prince had developed a reputation for being cruel, arrogant, and reckless. Surely logic would guide the Council's actions as they considered what was best for Er'Rets as a whole.

No one wanted a tyrant king. Right?

Both Bran and Sir Rigil Barak, the knight he served, supported Prince Oren for king. They often embarked upon quests for the elder prince—likely were doing so now. All Bran had said of his most recent trip was that he must go south on an urgent matter. Averella prayed Arman would keep them safe.

She took a moment to stretch and look around her. The rising sun cast a golden bloom over the vineyard, making the frost on the grapes shimmer like amethysts in the morning light. The sweet scent of grapes filled the crisp air. Dozens of people, bundled in warm cloaks, hats, and gloves, worked the snow-covered rows in a swift, precise rhythm. Their breath clouded above their heads, while straw baskets sat at their feet, waiting to catch their sweet offerings. Shears clinked, leaves rustled, and grass crunched underfoot. Low hums of conversation and the occasional burst of laughter rose over the steady sound of work. They had been at it since midnight, working with lanterns to light the way. Now that day had broken, the sun peeked over the horizon, white gold against a sky swirling with pink and lilac clouds.

Breathtaking.

Averella turned back to her row, still heavy with clusters of frozen grapes. She reached for one, snapped it free, and moved quickly to the next. The sooner they finished, the sooner Master Pytel could begin pressing and Averella could thaw herself by a warm fire.

Another hour or so passed before the last basket was emptied into the cart, and Master Pytel declared them finished. A hearty cheer rose up across the now-barren field, and the people began to disperse: Master Pytel's crew to the winery, peasants to their homes, and servants, along with Averella, to the stronghold.

The enormity of Granton Castle made it nearly impossible to heat well in winter, so even when Averella went inside, she felt no warmth until she reached her chambers. She quickly closed the door behind her and walked straight toward the fireplace, grateful for its heat. She removed mittens stained purple from the harvest, then both sets of gloves she had worn beneath. Her fingers were red, and she stretched them toward the fire.

The door to her chambers opened, and her sister, Gypsum, slipped inside, a thick, grey shawl tucked around her shoulders. The neutral color only enhanced Gypsum's golden curls and the natural flush of her baby pink cheeks.

"Have fun, did you?" she asked.

Averella wiggled her stiff hands above the flames. "Worth every frost-bitten finger."

"You're mad, you know." Gypsum came to stand beside her, pursing her full lips. The elder of her little sisters at twelve already stood eye-to-eye with Averella. The girl was a true beauty. All four of Averella's little sisters were the loveliest young ladies in all Er'Rets, next to their cousin Tara, of course. Averella, however, pale with thin dark hair, looked nothing like them. The only thing she had in her favor was the title she would one day inherit from her mother.

"It was a bountiful harvest," Averella said. "One of the best we have seen in years." And if that did not impress Gypsum... "It will bring in a great deal of money."

"Mother will be pleased by that outcome."

"Indeed she will." Averella rubbed her hands together. They were still icy cold but starting to tingle, which was a good sign. She would thaw soon enough.

The door burst open, and both girls turned. Syrah rushed inside, wide-eyed, her braided brown hair frizzing outward like that of a stray cat caught unaware. In her dash, she left the door gaping behind her.

"Syrah, the heat." Gypsum ran and closed the door.

"Sorry!" Syrah gasped in a breath and extended a piece of parchment toward Averella, shook it. "I found this nailed to the door of the temple. Read it. Quickly!"

Though Averella's still-cold fingers protested, she managed to take hold of the parchment. A sense of foreboding crept through her as she angled it toward the hearth for an extra bit of light and read.

I hereby announce the forthcoming marriage between Prince Gidon Hadar of Sitna and Lady Averella Amal of Carmine. This is the first public notice. If anyone knows of any just cause or impediment why these two persons should not be joined together in Holy Matrimony, you are to declare it.

Signed,

Chora Tally

Averella reeled. Heat shot through her, dispelling the remaining fatigue from her nocturnal labor. "The nerve of that man. Does he honestly think this will work?"

Gypsum tugged the parchment away and read it while Averella paced before the hearth.

"I thought it strange too, my lady," Syrah said. "I mean, men do this often enough, but I would think a prince could come himself or at the very least, send an envoy."

Averella gestured to the parchment. "What men propose this way?"

"Lots," Syrah said. "They hang an engagement announcement on the door of the local temple. As long as no one complains, they can marry the girl."

Averella found this unsurprising, but that it could happen to her, the daughter of a duchess...

"That's rather unromantic," Gypsum said.

"There is little romance in most marriages," Syrah said. "Sometimes a girl doesn't even meet her groom before she takes her vows. The parents work it all out."

Averella sank onto the armchair near the hearth. "I cannot imagine anything more dreadful."

"You've led a singular life, my lady," Syrah said. "For most of us, if a husband and wife are lucky, they'll at least become friends during their marriage."

"Well, I do hope if Jonol gets the urge to marry he will ask you himself," Averella said, speaking of the young guardsman courting Syrah.

Syrah grinned and fingered her apron. "I hope so too."

"Vrella, I'm confused," Gypsum said, still frowning at the announcement. "I thought the prince already asked you to marry him."

Averella wrung her hands and grimaced. "Not officially. Lord Nathak broached the subject with Mother last spring. And Gidon has hinted on several occasions. Declared it to some while I have been close enough to hear him. I had hoped that my personal rebuffs would have been enough to dissuade him by now, but apparently not. He once told Silvo Hamartano that when he and I were married, he would move the vineyards away from Granton Castle so that he would not have to look on the servants who worked them."

"*Move* the vineyards?" Gypsum said.

"What did you say when he did that?" Syrah asked Averella.

"Gidon is a fool. I ignored him."

"But Averella, this is serious." Gypsum handed back the parchment. "You cannot ignore it. In fact, you must show Mother right away."

Dutiful as ever, Gypsum was, but Averella could not deny the girl was right. If only her engagement to Bran had been announced already. Then she would not be in this mess. "Yes, I suppose I must."

She sighed, wishing she could toss the parchment into the flames and be done with Gidon Hadar as quickly as it would burn. Unfortunately, it looked like she was going to have to get help if she was to put off the Crown Prince once and for all because this proposal did not only affect Averella, it affected all of Carm Duchy.

2

"Should I be worried?" Averella paused in her pacing long enough to face the jade desk in her mother's private study. The duchess was reading the announcement yet again, the top of which she had weighted against the desk with a cast iron paperweight of a wolfhound puppy. She still wore a robe over her nightdress, her auburn hair long and curling loose around her stern-set face.

"Of course not, dearest," Mother said. "This isn't the first proposal we've rejected."

Too true. There had been four unwelcome proposals thus far, not including the myriad of hints from Gidon Hadar. And of course, Bran's suit, which still sat unanswered. The reminder set Averella pacing again. Her gaze slipped to the changing screen in the corner that hid the entrance to one of the many secret passageways in the castle. She longed to slip up to the top of Ryson Tower and check the roads for signs of Bran's return. She prayed he might be on his way home this moment.

"Once Anillo returns with Father Sangee, we'll soon have this set to rights," Mother said.

Averella moved to the southwestern-facing window and looked down. She could clearly see the entrance to the castle and the normal early morning comings and goings, but no steward or priest were yet in sight. How long did it take two men to walk across the castle grounds?

"These greedy men all want one thing, and it is not me," Averella said. "They want rule of Carm Duchy and the wealth that comes with it." As Mother's heir, Averella would one day take control of it.

And those men wanted control of Averella.

Gidon included.

"Do not grow agitated, Averella. You know I will not marry you off to just anyone."

Averella thanked Arman for the blessing of a Mother who understood. Had her father still been alive, he would have accepted one of Averella's suitors long ago.

Averella glanced at the painting of Ice Island that hung in the center of the brownstone chimney behind Mother's desk. Her uncle Verdot, warden of Ice Island, had all but promised Averella's hand to Nash Erlichman, the son of a wealthy businessman from Tsaftown.

"Why do you like this painting so much?" Averella asked. "I cannot look at it without thinking about Uncle Verdot and his ambitious friend."

Mother turned her gaze to the painting, and her expression grew nostalgic. "It reminds me that if not for the grace of Arman, I could be incarcerated there myself."

Averella wrinkled her nose. "What crime could you have possibly committed that is worthy of such a place?"

Mother pinned her with an arresting stare. "I am not trying to be droll. All of us are sinners, Averella. Some bent on evil more than others, but we all deserve death." She looked back to the painting, her brow pinched. "Yet some within those walls are innocent, did you know that?"

"Locked away for something one did not do? Surely not."

"Oh, yes. It's a terrible fact." Mother sighed and turned back to the announcement on her desk. "How unfortunate that Prince Gidon is so much more persistent than your other suitors have been."

Averella's lips curled in a grimace. "And exceedingly more revolting."

Mother chuckled. "I wish I could disagree."

"There is only one man I wish to marry, as you well know."

"I do well know, my dear, but I caution you not to mention Master Rennan in the presence of Father Sangee. He will not approve."

Averella moved to the window that looked out over the bailey and the northern road. The temple sat just inside the castle walls. "Why did you invite Father Sangee here, anyway?"

"Because the proposal was posted at the temple. He knows about it, and we must make sure he hears our refusal clearly."

Averella supposed that made sense.

Another quarter of an hour passed before a knock on the door proceeded the arrival of Anillo, Mother's steward and Shield, escorting Father Sangee.

As always, the priest wore a white hooded cloak over a white tunic and black trousers. The hood was down, revealing a crop of gray hair tied in a short tail. "What is the emergency?" he asked. "I have a service to prepare."

Mother moved the paperweight and extended the announcement. Anillo accepted the parchment from her hand and passed it to Father Sangee.

The priest took a moment to read it, and declared, "But this is delightful! I always knew Lady Averella would make a fine match."

"I will *not* marry Gidon Hadar," Averella said.

Father Sangee's pale eyes met hers. "Why ever not?"

Averella could name a hundred reasons, but she started with one he should understand deeply. "He does not follow Arman."

"He was devoted at our temple as a child and is officially a member of the Armanite faith," Father Sangee said. "On *my* roster."

Sitna did not have a Temple Arman. "Only because the succession to the throne is limited to 'the Heirs of Armanite body,'" Averella said, quoting the Basic Law of Er'Rets. "He does not really believe. Nor is he a follower in The Way."

The priest set his jaw. "Is this why your family attends services so rarely, Your Grace? Do you follow the sect, as well?"

"The temple of Arman is in his people," Mother said.

Father Sangee frowned. "Prince Gidon Hadar will be our king, and very soon."

To the great detriment of them all, Averella thought but wisely refrained from speaking it aloud. "Yet I do not wish to be queen."

The priest's mouth gaped. "Your Grace, do you agree with this?"

"Who Averella marries is her choice," Mother said. "And I am already in negotiations with another."

"Who?" the priest asked.

Mother raised her chin. "I am not yet at liberty to say, but I am on the verge of accepting."

Hope surged inside Averella. She knew Bran had spoken with Mother, but negotiations sounded so very official and final. She wanted to hug her mother and cheer.

The priest turned his attention back on Averella. "And you mean to refuse the prince, my lady? Truly?"

Averella nodded. "Indeed. I do not love him."

"This is most irregular," Father Sangee said. "Much here today has surprised me greatly."

"I felt it imperative that you hear my objection to this proposal," Mother said. "I do not grant permission for Averella to marry Prince Gidon. My answer is no."

Father Sangee bowed deeply. "You have been heard clearly, Your Grace."

"Will you sign your witness to this letter?" Mother procured a new scroll and weighted it open on the jade desktop. Anillo stepped in and moved her quill and ink beside the parchment.

Father Sangee's eyes widened slightly, but he approached the table, leaned down, and read the scroll. "Yes, I will sign as witness." He made quick use of the quill. "I do feel terribly awkward about the entire situation. That this announcement was posted at the temple concerns me. Will the prince come here expecting a wedding?"

"I will bloodvoice Lord Nathak right away and give him my answer," Mother said.

"Ah, yes. I see. That will do splendidly, of course. Thank you, Your Grace." Again, the priest bowed.

"I thank you for hearing my objection so swiftly," Mother said. "Good day, Father Sangee."

"Ah... Yes, good day." The priest bowed a third time, then took a step in the wrong direction.

"This way, Father." Anillo gestured to the door.

"Thank you, sir."

And they left.

At the sound of their footsteps retreating, the tension eased from Averella's shoulders, and she turned her focus to her mother. "You meant Bran, did you not? When you said you were negotiating with another?"

"I *did*... but I have not fully decided, so do not rush ahead and make assumptions."

Averella wanted to do just that. Instead, she sank onto the chaise lounge against the far wall, glad the visit with the priest was over. "When will you message Lord Nathak?"

"Right now, if you'll give me a moment."

Averella pursed her lips and watched as her mother closed her eyes. The gifted did not *need* to close their eyes to bloodvoice, but Mother said it was polite to do so. She also said it helped with concentration.

Averella had been practicing, to little avail. Just a few weeks ago she had awakened in the night to the sound of people talking in her room. Only there had been no one present. She had brushed it off as the dregs of a dream until the same thing happened at breakfast. When she told her mother about hearing the voices, the duchess had been delighted to pronounce Averella gifted in the bloodvoicing magic. She taught her to shield and forbade her to experiment with her ability until she had been properly trained.

It had been shocking, really. Averella had always heard those with the gift showed potential at a much younger age. She had given little thought to it ever happening to her.

Until it had.

Averella understood little about her mother's powers, but she had heard Sir Gavin call Mother a Veil Warrior, which was a magical bloodvoice legend from stories told by minstrels.

Averella had no desire to become a legend. All she had ever wanted in life was simply to create hybrid plants and vines, marry Bran, and do her best to keep Carm Duchy and its vineyards running successfully.

Mother sighed so loudly that Averella looked up. She found her mother slouched, elbows on the desk, hands cupping her face.

Averella winced. "It went well, I gather?"

"He debated me, as usual," Mother said. "That man is delusional about his level of charm."

"But he understood you, did he not?"

"He did. And he swears he will change my mind when he arrives here."

Averella's hand flew to her mouth as she processed this unexpected turn of events. "They are coming here?"

"They are."

Averella leapt from the chaise lounge and gazed out the southern windows. The road appeared empty. She wished Bran were here. He had a way of stating logical truths that always calmed her nerves. "What will we do?"

"I will prepare to receive them," Mother said. "You will attend the service at Father Sangee's temple this morning, then remain there until I send for you."

"Remain at the Temple Arman?"

"You will be safe there, dearest. Even though the prince sent his man to post the announcement on the temple door, I daresay none of them have any intention of attending service."

"But I am not an Armanite."

Mother leveled a glance at Averella. "The Armanite faith is part of our history. While the theological differences between us and them cannot be ignored, we both serve Arman. With the right attitude, I'm sure you will enjoy the experience."

Averella sighed, unable to think up a reason to refuse. "I will dress for service then, and perhaps pack a bag in case I must take sanctuary there."

"A wise idea," Mother said. "Bring Syrah with you. When you are ready to depart, I will have Anillo and two guardsmen escort you there. And keep your mind shielded. Lord Nathak might try to look through your eyes to find you."

Averella shivered. "That is rather terrifying."

"Yes, but if you are shielded, he will fail. I do wish we'd had time to teach you to use your magic, but at least I know you can shield well."

Averella swallowed her fear, well aware of what such precautions meant. Gidon Hadar might not accept this latest rejection at all. He might try to force her to marry him.

Averella trusted her mother implicitly, but living in a world where men discounted women at every turn, Averella—like her mother—would be sure to have a contingency plan, just in case.

3

Syrah's elbow to Averella's ribs jolted her awake. She inhaled the musty aroma of aged oak and blinked at the candles flickering on the altar behind Father Sangee, whose monotone voice reverberated to the high ceiling of the Temple Arman.

Merciful heart! The man was *still* speaking. This was his fourth or fifth trip to the podium. She had lost count. She did not recall so many teachings upon her last visit, though Father Sangee's droning tone made him a monotonous orator.

Perhaps he was trying to emulate the chanting Armanite hymns with his speech.

The Temple Arman was segregated by gender with separate entrances for men and women. Averella and Syrah sat on the left-hand side of the sanctuary with a young adherent named Elzea. The girl wore a simple brown linen dress with a white linen wimple over her hair. She had large brown eyes and a ready smile. Father Sangee had assigned her to oversee Averella's visit. He likely wanted to make sure Averella did nothing foolish, like tread upon the men's side of the temple.

Again, Averella wished Bran were home. What possible quest could Prince Oren find so important to keep him and Sir Rigil away for so long? Some corruption within the Council, no doubt. Or perhaps something to do with the warring giant tribes in the Nahar forest.

Arman, I need him back. Please return Bran to me.

It was too early, though. At a minimum, such trips usually took Bran away for two months, and he had been gone this time only three weeks.

No, Averella could not put her hope in Bran Rennan or even her mother. Should Prince Gidon arrive with an army set upon forcing her into marriage, she must be ready with a plan of her own. She would not put it past him to coerce her by harming the people of Carm, or worse, her sisters.

Averella must thwart every dastardly scheme she could imagine Prince Gidon capable of trying in his quest to have his way. As soon as this service ended, she would write her mother a letter and suggest she move Gypsum, Mariel, Rioja, and Terra to a place of safety.

Many things about the Armanite service were different from Teshuwah, which was the holy day gathering for believers of The Way. Followers met in homes, a practice Averella found more intimate and meaningful than listening to a series of speeches. Father Sangee had not presented encouragement from the Book of Life, either. He merely quoted famous pontiffs and medial priests of old, as if their ancient words were somehow more revered than those from Arman's holy book.

Suddenly, everyone was standing, so Averella pushed to her feet. Was it over? But no. Father Sangee was saying something about obedience. Averella should have tried harder to listen. Mother would undoubtedly be disappointed when she had no remarks on Father Sangee's teaching.

Teachings.

Now everyone was kneeling, so Averella did the same. She could not help notice that some of the men across the aisle wore no shoes. Averella frowned and glanced at Elzea's feet, but the adherent was not barefoot. What did *that* mean?

When the service finally came to an end, Elzea led them back to the library, where Averella had been enjoying some of the old books earlier that morning while Elzea and Syrah sewed.

Averella found pen and parchment, quickly wrote a letter to her mother about getting her sisters to safety, and sent a page to deliver it. Then she joined the other girls in a group of chairs before a large picture window overlooking the now-empty vineyard. Syrah had resumed her embroidery while Elzea mended a tear in one of Father Sangee's robes.

Averella had brought along her embroidery basket, of course, but she detested embroidery almost as much as she hated Prince Gidon, so while the others worked, she set about untangling her different colors of thread.

"Why did some of the men remove their shoes for the service?" she asked.

"I was curious about that too," Syrah said.

"They are sojourners," Elzea said. "Recent converts or some who have returned to devotion after falling away. They don't feel worthy to carry their failures into the temple, so they leave them at the door."

Syrah frowned. "Because your failures are on the bottoms of your feet?"

"It's symbolic," Elzea said, taking a stitch in the white fabric pooled on her lap.

"I rather like that," Averella said as she worked to untangle a green strand of thread from a snarl of black. "I am glad that both the Armanite faith and believers in The Way welcome newcomers and those who have gone astray."

"Why are there so many sermons?" Syrah asked.

"There are five teachings," Elzea said. "Five is a holy number in the Armanite faith."

"What an effective way to get the message across," Syrah said, brightly.

Averella did not know about that. "What made you want to join the—ah..." She winced as an ache bit into her temple. "Join Temple Arman as an adherent?"

"Are you all right, my lady?" Syrah asked.

"Just a headache," Averella said.

Elzea frowned as she gazed out the window. "That's similar to your reason for being here today," she said. "My father wanted me to marry."

Syrah huffed. "Why do fathers insist on betrothing their daughters to the most odious men?"

"Oh, Benjen isn't odious," Elzea said. "He and I had been friends for many years. Our parents are friends. He said he loved me, and I do love him like a brother. But I couldn't imagine yoking myself to him in such a way."

"That must have been difficult," Averella said, wincing as the headache again stabbed into her temples. She might need to see about getting a cup of chamomile tea. "Was he angry when you came here?"

Elzea chuckled. "Benjen or my father?"

Averella shrugged as she tugged the last of the green thread from the tangle of black. "Both, I guess." She dropped the threads in her lap and rubbed her finger against the pain in her temple.

"Father said I was a silly girl and that I must marry Benjen or join the temple," Elzea said. "Benjen said I broke his heart. Said he would never marry."

"How sad," Syrah said.

"Yes," Elzea said. "So, you see, I can relate to your plight, my lady. I hope it is easier for you to reject the prince than it was for me to reject Benjen."

"It has been no hardship at all," Averella said. "The prince is not my friend."

"Plus, this isn't Lady Averella's first proposal," Syrah said. "She's rather proficient at rejecting suitors."

"Syrah!" Averella shot her a warning look.

"Oh, do tell me the story," Elzea said.

"Not one story," Syrah said, "but five. Six, if you count the prince."

Elzea seemed to have forgotten her mending. "Six proposals!"

Averella sighed. Only one proposal had held any interest for her. Though she supposed they had nothing better to do at the moment. She might as well harvest her personal life as a source of entertainment.

She set aside her embroidery kit, stood, and walked to the window. Outside, the rows of recently-picked vines stood orderly, their once-laden branches now stripped of fruit, basking in the golden afternoon sunlight. In the distance, far past the great expanse of fields and farms that embodied the duchy of Carm, the land gradually rose to meet the Chowmah Mountains, draped in the ominous, thick black cloud of Darkness. Averella hated the way Darkness loomed, as if brooding and biding its time while it exuded a foreboding sense of unease.

She told Elzea about Captain Mercer proposing to her at Father's funeral and Uncle Verdot's friend Joonas Erlichman, proposing on behalf of his son Nash. "Then there was Lord Coble from Land's End."

"Where the black knights are from?" Elzea asked.

"The very place," Syrah said.

"How frightening!" Elzea said. "I cannot imagine having to live in Darkness."

Averella again glanced to the distant mountain chain shrouded in dark clouds. "Lord Coble actually asked to marry Mother first," she said, "but in the event Mother did not wish to remarry, he suggested a match with me. Mother had no interest in an alliance with the man suspected of training black knights, so she rejected him without even telling me about it until months later."

"Then there was Master Yarden," Syrah piped in.

"Yes, Davel Yarden, bachelor brother to Lord Yarden of Mitspah has proposed *three* times," Averella said, coming back to sit down in her chair. Just thinking of Master Yarden made her sigh. "Every year on his own birthday he urges me to give him the gift of my hand in marriage."

"How odd," Elzea said.

"All of them want nothing but to control Carm Duchy through Lady Averella," Syrah said.

"But with the prince, that only comes to five," Elzea said. "Who is the sixth?"

"She is sworn to secrecy," Syrah said, batting her eyes.

"Only because I already accepted," Averella said.

"Who?" Elzea grinned and slipped to the edge of her chair.

Averella pictured Bran's face in her mind. His sandy hair and deep brown eyes. His fair complexion, often sunburned because he never remembered to wear the salve she made him. He exuded kindness and strength yet had a hint of defiance in his expression. Averella knew that came from the juxtaposition of his intelligence set against the vulnerability of his status as a lesser noble. He had worked hard for his place as squire to Sir Rigil yet constantly endured ridicule from peers who thought they had superior bloodlines.

"I am not permitted to reveal his name," she finally said. "My mother swore me to secrecy until she could work out the details. We do not want anyone trying to thwart or take advantage of the situation."

"Your mother accepted the offer, then?" Elzea asked.

"Not officially," Averella said. "It is complicated. He is not titled. He comes from a lesser family and has not been trained in politics. That adds challenges when you consider my inheritance."

"Oh, I see," Elzea said. "Will you at least tell me about the proposal? Did he speak to your mother?"

"He did," Averella said, "but only after he spoke to me."

"In the vineyard under a full moon," Syrah crooned.

Elzea's eyes grew wide. "Truly?"

"Yes, we often walk together in the vineyard," Averella said. "I have a favorite place there where I keep some special plant projects. It is a hobby of mine to graft plants together to see what can grow. I was showing him my most recent creation when he knelt in the grass."

A little gasp from Elzea. "He knelt down?"

Syrah giggled. "Wait until you hear what he said."

"Yes, well, I thought he had dropped something," Averella said, smiling at the memory, "so I crouched to help him find it. Then he took my hands in his and said—Averella lowered her voice to mimic Bran all while Syrah dramatically mouthed along the words they had both memorized—'Dearest Averella, I have these past two years endeavored to become worthy of you. The skilled hands of the master vigneron, Arman, has been slowly grafting our lives together. In the shadow of these vines with the moon and stars above as witness, I find the courage to ask for your hand. Will you give me the honor of grafting my life to yours, that we might create a bond that withstands the tests of time and bears the sweetest of fruits?'"

Elzea's mouth gaped open. "He said all that?"

Averella beamed, loving the girl's reaction to the story. "He did."

"You can believe her," Syrah said. "She's not one to embellish."

"And you accepted?" Elzea asked.

"I did," Averella said, "on the condition that he speak to my mother. Which he did. And then I spoke to her. And now we are waiting to see what will be done." She slumped back in her chair. "I have not seen him since that night. He has gone off on a trip and will not return for several more weeks. I am hopeful that by then, Mother will have an answer for us both."

"If your Benjen had given a proposal like that, might you have accepted?" Syrah asked.

"I would have laughed myself silly," Elzea said. "Such words would have sounded ridiculous coming from him."

"Did he not ask you himself?" Averella asked.

"The second time he did. He said, Zea, what's this nonsense I hear about you refusing to marry me?' But the first time, he asked my father, who accepted on my behalf."

"How like men to assume women will, of course, agree with anything they decide for us," Syrah said.

"Yes, well, I've always known marriage is not for me." Elzea leaned forward and whispered. "I would not like the marriage act."

Averella frowned. "The contract?"

Elzea swallowed and glanced over her shoulder, as if someone might have materialized through the closed door. Still whispering, she said, "What it takes to produce a child."

"Oh!" Averella chuckled. "Consummation, you mean? How do you know you would not like it?"

Elzea straightened and nearly fell off her chair.

"Averella!" Syrah rolled her eyes. "Such words."

"Sorry," Averella said, fighting back a smile. "I meant no offense."

"Nor I," whispered Elzea. "But...have you never seen sheep mate out in the fields? It's shocking."

Averella pursed her lips and fought back a snort, but a look from Syrah set them both into a fit of giggles. Elzea quickly joined in the laughter.

A knock on the door made Elzea squeak, and this time, she did fall off her chair, which only made Averella and Syrah laugh harder. Elzea caught herself on the arm of the chair, though, and quickly went to open the door.

Father Sangee stood out in the hallway, and the girls quickly sobered.

"My lady, you have a visitor," he said. "He is waiting in the parlor."

He? "Who is it?" Averella asked.

A faint furrow formed between Father Sangee's brows. With a quick glance to the side, he shifted his weight from one foot to the other, then finally met Averella's gaze head-on and uttered, "The man said it was an urgent matter from the castle."

"It's probably a page with a reply from your mother," Syrah said,

"Oh, good point." Averella smiled at the priest. "Please tell him I will come right away."

Father Sangee's gaze flitted nervously from one girl to the next. "Very well." Then he walked away.

Elzea shut the door and leaned back against it. She made the sign of the hand, pressing her palm to her heart, then kissing her lips.

But when she looked from Averella to Syrah, they all burst into laughter.

4

"How is your headache?" Syrah asked as the duo made their way down the hall toward the parlor in the front of the temple. It was the only co-ed room in the building besides the segregated sanctuary and dining hall.

"It seems to have gone," Averella said. "I am grateful. It was most unpleasant."

Syrah opened the parlor door for Averella. At first, the room seemed empty as Averella and Syrah walked straight to the warmth of the fireplace. At the sound of the door closing behind them, both turned and looked, not upon a page, but upon Chora Talley, Prince Gidon's steward.

The hairs rose on Averella's arms. Father Sangee had not warned her. Why?

Chora, a man in his late twenties, was short and soft around the middle. He had cropped brown hair, a pear-like nose, and wore brown robes.

He bowed politely. "Lady Averella, might we speak privately?"

"No, we cannot," Averella said.

"Oh, I see." He took one tentative step toward them, then seemed to think better of such a tactic. "Shall I just deliver my message in front of your maid?"

"If you must," Averella said. "Though you could always choose silence."

He inhaled a long breath until his chest puffed out. "I'm afraid I cannot remain silent, my lady. Nothing to do but the task set before me." This last part he mumbled to himself, as if to inspire courage.

Oh dear.

The man approached and lowered himself to both knees, which made his robes billow out in the most unflattering manner. He reached for her hands, which Averella tucked behind her.

"Ahh." Master Talley jerked back his own hands, as if burned. "Um... My esteemed lady, my master, His Majesty Prince Gidon Hadar, our future king, has sent me with a most heartfelt and urgent message."

Merciful heart. This was ridiculous. "Has he? Why not come himself?"

"He is at the moment, indisposed," Master Talley said. "Yet, I am well, and so I've come."

"Yes, we see you here before us, Master Talley," Averella said. "Do say what you have come to say and be done with it."

"Yes, well, I carry with me a most precious gift," Master Talley said. "His Majesty has chosen you to be his bride. Isn't that wonderful? As you see, I've come as an extension of his arm to convey his decision that you marry him at once."

Averella folded her arms over her chest. "Was there a question to be answered, Master Talley?"

The man frowned. "Wasn't there?"

"I heard none," Syrah said.

"Nor I," Averella added. "You said you have come to convey his decision. Forgive me if I misunderstand, but I was raised to believe a marriage decision requires the consent of two persons."

Chora's thick eyebrows sank over his eyes. "Yes, that's why I've come. To hear your answer."

"Oh, good," Averella said. "I thought for a moment that I might not be permitted to answer at all."

Master Talley huffed and shifted on his knees, readjusting his robe. "Please, my lady, what is your answer?"

This poor, pathetic man. What a horrible job he had. "My answer is no."

His eyes widened. "No?"

"Your ears do you credit, sir," Averella said.

He sputtered. "But you cannot say no."

"I believe I just did."

"I heard her as well," Syrah added.

"But I... I cannot go back to him with such an answer. It will ruin a perfectly good day."

What an odd man. "While I empathize with your plight, Master Tally, I am unwilling to pledge my life to that man in order to ensure you have a good day."

"That man is your future king!"

"He is not my king yet, sir." And Averella prayed fervently that he never would be. His uncle, Prince Oren, was far more qualified. And merciful. And sane. "Is there more to the message?" she asked. "If not, I have matters to attend to, as I am sure you do as well."

Master Talley sat back on his heels. At first, he looked completely bewildered, but then he clenched his jaw, squared his shoulders, and rose again to his knees. "I beg you reconsider, my lady. His Majesty is not accustomed to rejection of any kind. I shudder to think of how he may respond. Besides, marrying him will make you queen of all Er'Rets. Won't that be nice? You could live in the south where it is much warmer and Armanite temples abound."

"I am afraid your notion of 'nice' falls short of my expectations for a meaningful partnership," Averella snapped. "I have no wish of a royal position nor am I a member of the Armanite faith. His Majesty's response is of little concern to me. I am sorry that you must convey my rejection as it will no doubt cause you discomfort from your disappointed master, but I have no interest in sacrificing my freedom and dignity to profit Gidon Hadar. I will not marry him. Ever. Good day to you, sir." Averella grabbed Syrah's arm and dragged her around where Master Talley knelt on the floor.

The man grunted behind them, and as Averella opened the door, she caught sight of him pushing to his feet.

"You will regret this, my lady," he called after her. "Remember my words."

While Averella could not imagine ever forgetting this terribly award scene, Chora Talley was wrong. She would never regret rejecting Gidon Hadar, even if that meant she had to do so daily for the rest of her life. She would never take the name of Hadar as her own.

As Averella and Syrah made their way back toward the library, Averella's thoughts raced along with her heart. "Of all the ridiculous notions," she said.

"My lady, I can't believe it," Syrah said.

"I wish I could say the same. What if my mother is unable to rebuff the prince's advances?"

"I'm sure that won't be the case."

Averella twisted her hands. "I know she will do all she can, but I put nothing past Prince Gidon and Lord Nathak. I must be ready."

"What will you do?"

They entered the library and found Elzea gone. Averella closed the door and quickly peeked down the three short aisles of bookshelves. All empty. They were alone.

"Elzea dedicated her life to service in the temple Arman to avoid marriage," Averella said. "I see no reason why I could not do the same."

Syrah folded her arms and pinned Averella with a doubtful stare. "An adherent? You?"

"At least for a time. I would only be pretending."

Syrah frowned. "But if you dedicate your life to the temple, you must give up your inheritance, which means Lady Gypsum will rule Carm and the prince will set his sights on her."

Averella's stomach sank. "You are wise to have come to that conclusion, Syrah. I must know if my sisters are safe before I do anything that might forsake them."

"Surely your mother will soon answer the letter you sent this morning."

Averella hoped so. She had packed a bag before coming to the temple. She had not brought it with her, though, not wanting to alarm Father Sangee. She had no such concerns now. "I want to know why Father Sangee concealed the truth that Chora Talley had come to see me."

"I find that strange, as well," Syrah said. "Might he be on Prince Gidon's side? And if so, why?"

Averella thought about it. "Perhaps the prince promised him money. Or favors. It is also clear he believes Gidon Hadar has the right to rule and cares not that he purchased his membership in the temple and does not really believe."

"What will you do?" Syrah asked.

"Wait to find out about my sisters' safety and send for my packed bag. I am still deciding where I might flee. Do not be alarmed if I keep it from you. The less you know, the better."

"My lady, please. I can take care of myself."

"In the meantime," Averella said, her tone firm, "I must ask Elzea to take me to Father Sangee. I will tell him I wish to serve Arman as temporary adherent and see if I might discover his true motives."

"I will find Elzea and send for your bag," Syrah said.

While Syrah left on her errands, Averella had no choice but to bide her time. She thought over the many cities in which she might hide and realized there were few options open to her. Mother's birthplace of

Tsaftown was the obvious option. Averella's grandparents lived there and many cousins. It would be the first place Prince Gidon would search, though, and as such, could not be seriously considered.

Zerah Rock might have been a good option if Sir Rigil were at home and could see to her welfare. With him off on a quest with Bran, Averella would be at the mercy of his mother, Lady Zora, a woman Averella had never liked much. She could not go to Mitspah where Davel Yarden would be sure to propose yet again. Nor could she trust the Levy family in Mahanaim. Lord Levy, who served on the Council of Seven with her mother, loyally supported Prince Gidon in all matters.

Averella knew no one in the south truly well except for Prince Oren's daughter Glassea... The idea kindled into flame. Of course! She could visit Glassea in Armonguard. What better place to stay safe from Prince Gidon than with the uncle so many hoped would rule in his stead?

But first she must create a diversion.

Averella sat at the desk and withdrew a fresh sheet of parchment. She started a letter to her cousin, Tara, letting her know that she would soon pay a visit to Tsaftown. Averella crossed out several lines and finally abandoned the letter, even crumpling it. She did not throw it away, however, nor did she pen another. She had no intention of sending such a letter at all. She only wanted to leave this clue so that someone might think she had written and sent a final draft.

She then wrote a second letter, this time to her Aunt Revada in Tsaftown. She confessed a desire to convert to the Armanite faith and her interest in to learning more about becoming a loyal adherent. She claimed her mother was against the idea and asked her aunt whether service to Arman was worth forfeiting her birthright.

This letter she also did not send but abandoned beside the crumpled draft to cousin Tara.

Syrah returned with Elzea, who insisted on taking them to a room if they were going to stay the night. Averella gathered the ink, parchment, and the drafts of her letters.

Elzea led them to a narrow attic room on the third floor. It held two cot-like beds separated by a small table beneath a dormer window that looked out over the vineyards. Elzea left them there to get settled and went to inquire about a meeting with Averella and Father Sangee.

"Well, this is cozy," Averella said, setting the ink, parchment, and letters on the table.

Not long after, Averella's packed bag arrived with a letter from her mother, sealed in wax with Mother's signet ring. She read the letter aloud to Syrah.

Averella,

I am pleased you are enjoying your visit to the Temple Arman, though I do counsel against your idea of becoming an adherent. You can do so much more for Arman and your people as Duchess of Carm than you can as a temple adherent.

I was surprised to get word of thieves in the area, though we have only encountered one of their number, thus far. I assure you, our gold has been protected and will not be discovered, no matter how many more thieves arrive. Besides, Captain Loam has set up sentries at the gate and will inform me at once should he notice anything suspicious.

It is lonely here without you. I look forward to the end of your visit there and your return to my household.

Love,

Mother

"What does it mean?" Syrah asked.

"She understands me," Averella said. "We met the first thief, who was Master Talley. Prince Gidon and his men are in the area. My golden-haired sisters are safely tucked away. And Captain Loam and the army are on alert."

"Oh, I see."

"You must keep hold of this letter and those drafts I have written." Averella gestured to the table. "They will stand as proof of my wishes, should Mother need—"

A knock at the door. "My lady? It's me," Elzea said.

Syrah let in the adherent. "Well?"

"Brother Milton said Father Sangee is too busy to speak with you today. He begs you try again tomorrow."

"He puts me off when it is not yet midday?" Averella said. "What could possibly keep him too busy to have a word with me?"

Elzea frowned. "Father Sangee has many responsibilities."

"I am sure he does," Averella said, "but surely he can spare me a moment. Come, Syrah. We shall inquire of Father Sangee ourselves."

Elzea reluctantly led Averella and Syrah to the threshold of the men's wing where two male adherents stood guard.

"Please inform Father Sangee that Lady Averella Amal must speak with him on a matter of some urgency," Averella said.

"He's not to be disturbed," one of the men said.

"Then take my message to Brother Milton," Averella insisted.

"Yes, my lady."

The guard hurried away and returned with Brother Milton, a short medial priest in his mid-thirties with chin-length hair.

"Lady Averella," he said. "How may I be of service?"

"I wish to speak with Father Sangee, yet I am told he is unavailable."

"Yes, I'm sorry to say that is true," Brother Milton said.

"I do hope the man is not ill," Averella said. "Shall I send for my mother's physician?"

"No, no," Brother Milton said. "The father is perfectly well, just busy."

"Too busy for an urgent matter from the duchess's heir?" Averella asked.

Brother Milton swallowed and glanced at Syrah, then back to Averella. "I'm afraid so, my lady."

"I confess, I am shocked to hear this, Brother Milton. I am sure my mother will be, as well."

"Your Mother, as our patron, is held in high esteem, my lady," Brother Milton said, "but she is not above Arman."

"Of course not," Averella said. "Nor is Father Sangee above Arman, or dare I say, Prince Gidon."

Brother Milton coughed and swallowed. "Is there anything else you need, my lady?"

"I wish to do my part as a temporary adherent. I am considering dedicating my life but first want to make sure I can be an asset to Arman in this place. What orders do you think Father Sangee might have for me in this regard?"

"Oh, um, I'm sure you are welcome to stay as long as you contribute to the mission of the temple. Miss Elzea can direct your activities each day. Whatever she is assigned will be assigned to you, as well." He turned his attention to Syrah. "And you, miss?"

"I will do what my lady does," Syrah said.

"Very well," Brother Milton said. "Arman blesses you both for your service."

"Does he?" Averella asked. "How do you know?"

"I..." Brother Milton frowned. "He blesses all who serve him."

Syrah grabbed Averella's arm. "Come, my lady."

Averella sighed. She supposed there was nothing to do now but work and wait.

5

Two days passed by in which Averella and Syrah followed Elzea and the other adherents around the temple, living just as the other women did. They worshiped, prayed, read from the Book of Life, wrote letters to other temples, and journaled. They also helped bake bread and prepare food baskets for the poor. When Averella was not brooding about how Father Sangee was *still* avoiding her, she found the work fulfilling. She could imagine a permanent life here.

"Syrah," Averella said as they were arranging food into baskets, "if I had to remain in this temple forever, it would not be so bad. In fact, I think I would enjoy myself."

"Become a religious recluse?" Syrah asked.

"An anchoress," Averella said, liking the sound of it. "I would ask Mother to build a new place of worship and retreat known as the Women of the Way. All would vow to live a life of poverty and celibacy, to write letters, and to teach people about Arman and his son, Câan.

I could write a history of those devoted to Câan's teachings and The Way. Of course, we would also distribute bread to the poor, as well."

"Oh, of course."

"I would be an outspoken visionary. Our sisterhood would not be bound by laws but by the vow to be part of a philanthropic community of women who wish to serve Arman with their lives."

"The prince would not like it," Syrah said.

Averella grinned as she tucked a bushel of carrots into a basket. "Oh, he would despise it, which adds greatly to its appeal. I can hear him whining about how such charitable acts are depleting the treasury."

"What a dream such a life would be," Syrah mused. "If only you hadn't accepted Master Renan's proposal..."

Averella turned a pointed stare on her friend. "You mock me."

Syrah pressed her hand against her chest. "Me?"

"Of course I would prefer to marry Bran," Averella said. "It is only that such slow-paced living is conducive to active imaginings."

"Indeed," Syrah said. "I do hope we are not here much longer."

"If we are, I will start my book," Averella said, dreamily staring out the window at the garden.

The third morning shattered Averella's hopes of penning the exploits of Câan's followers as the adherents were awakened early for chores. This time, not to bake or prepare food, but to clean and complete needlework. Averella had to mop the kitchen floors and scrub the cushions of each and every pew. When she finally finished that, she was handed a needle and thread and asked to mend the clothing of the adherents and priests.

Averella loathed sewing.

If that was not bad enough, another horrible tension headache seized her, which made her hands tremble and her stitches uneven.

"Who assigns the daily tasks?" Averella asked Elzea.

"Father Sangee," Elzea said.

Figured. Well, Averella had no patience for such tedium.

Her sister, Gypsum, would undoubtedly make a stalwart adherent of the Armanite faith, but Averella now knew that such a life could never be for her.

That afternoon, her headache, blessedly, went away. By then Averella's fingers were pruned from scrubbing and blistered from pricks of the needle. Anillo came by with a report that Lord Nathak, Prince Gidon, and his Shield, Sir Kenton, had joined Master Talley as visitors of Granton Castle.

Averella paced before the fireplace in the parlor, frustrated by the prince's dogged stubbornness. "Do they mean to move in and simply take Granton Castle from my mother?"

"We do not believe they will stay long," Anillo said. "The prince is expected to make an appearance at a meeting in Mahanaim early next week. They will need to leave very soon in order to see that he arrives on time."

"Common sense would say so," Averella said, "but that particular group of men have never had any sense to speak of."

"My lady!" Syrah said. "You mustn't speak like that of the future king."

Averella glanced at the door. "It is only the three of us here," she said. "Who could I have offended by my words?"

"Just you remember that Father Sangee and his priests seem to be on their side," Syrah said.

True. While Averella had still not seen the head priest, Brother Milton had started a conversation with Averella at breakfast that made his allegiance clear.

"I wonder, my lady, why you won't at least consider the match? Imagine! A queen from Carmine. What a boon that would be."

When Averella asked the medial priest why he felt so strongly about the matter, all he would say was, *"Just think how such a role would enable you to help the people of Er'Rets."*

"I cannot speak for Brother Milton or any of the other priests," Averella said, "but Father Sangee is duty bound to accept my mother's decision. He signed his name as a witness to her refusal."

"I would not worry, my lady," Anillo said. "However, your mother did ask you to think about the possibility of a visit to Tsaftown to see your cousins."

Of all the silly ideas. "That is the first place he would look for me," she said. "He knows how much I love Tara." Which was why she had written the letters to her cousin and aunt, hoping to send the investigation on the wrong trail should she need to flee to Armonguard.

Which, unfortunately, was looking more necessary by the moment.

"Let me help, my lady," Syrah said. "I could put on your cloak and leave with Master Anillo. Perhaps the prince would see us and think you are leaving. In Tsaftown, I could visit my sister. It would be little hardship to see her again."

"That's not a bad idea," Anillo said.

"No, Syrah. I will not put you in harm's way," Averella said.

"How could I be harmed? Even if they gave chase, one look at me, and they'd realize they followed the wrong person."

"But if they believe you meant to deceive them, they might punish you," Averella said, "and there is no crueler man I know than Prince Gidon Hadar. It simply will not do." She lowered her voice. "Anillo, could you help me find a ship bound for Armonguard? There, I believe, I would truly be safe from the prince."

"How so?"

"I am friends with Lady Glassea. That gives me reason enough to visit. While I am there, I will beg the aid of Prince Oren and Lady Ginger, who surely will see the wisdom in keeping Carm Duchy out of Prince Gidon's control."

"I cannot argue with your logic, my lady," Anillo said. "I will check for ships, but I will also speak about this with your mother."

"Surely she will not refuse me," Averella said, for she could see no other way.

⤛⤜

Averella and Syrah took their meals in the temple dining hall. The walls and floors had been constructed of gray stone, and it always felt chilled despite the size of the blaze in the hearth. Long wooden tables stretched across the rectangular space with men and women seated separately.

Averella sat beside Syrah at a table with Elzea and some of the other adherents, enjoying a meal of barley soup and fresh bread, when Father Sangee approached.

Averella dabbed her mouth with her napkin. "Father Sangee," she said. "Do you have time to speak with me at last?"

His lips curved in a stiff smile. "Forgive me, no, my lady. A, uh, guest has arrived to see you."

Averella narrowed her eyes. "Not Master Talley, I hope?"

"No, my lady."

She stared at him, waiting. When the silence continued, Averella finally asked, "Who is it, then?"

"I... am not permitted to say," Father Sangee said.

Of all the nonsense! Averella took a deep breath. "Then I am not permitted to see this person."

He squared his shoulders. "My lady, I must object."

"No, you must not, Father," Averella said. "You will cease your machinations regarding my personal affairs. Is that clear?"

The priest's face reddened. "If that is your wish, my lady, though I will not take responsibility for the consequences." With that, he strode toward the exit, his robes puffing behind him.

A chill ran up Averella's arms. "What is that supposed to mean?" she asked Syrah.

"I don't know," Syrah said. "Perhaps we should go."

"I suppose we could take our dinner to our rooms," Averella said.

"Food is not allowed in your room," Elzea said.

"What would you have us do?" Syrah asked. "We can't just wait here for trouble to come."

"What trouble?" Elzea asked. "I'm sure Father Sangee will send the visitor away."

"He may *try*," Averella conceded, but she was not very confident that he would.

She was safe in the temple Arman, right? It mattered not whether Master Talley or Lord Nathak or even Prince Gidon himself came through that door. She would speak civilly and hold her ground.

"Well, if the father tried, he failed," Syrah said, nodding to the entrance.

Averella turned her gaze, and her heart dropped at the sight of Sir Kenton Garesh, Prince Gidon's Shield and protector, ducking under the door lintel. The man was the tallest Averella had ever seen who was not part giant. His arms, as thick as logs, greatly contrasted his long, fine hair, which draped over his shoulders like strings of fine black beads. Bran had admitted to her once that he hoped to never have to fight the man, though Averella knew that if Bran were here now, he would do everything he could to protect her.

The dining hall had only one entrance, which Sir Kenton currently blocked. Surely, he would not bother Averella with so many witnesses present?

He remained just inside the door, talking with Father Sangee, so Averella kept her head down and resumed eating. What else could she do?

Sooner or later, she would have to leave the dining hall, though. She would simply have to outlast Sir Kenton. Once he left, she would slip up to her room, then wait until dark and sneak away.

"He's coming," Syrah hissed.

Averella refused to allow any sort of emotion to reveal itself on her face. She tore off a piece of bread, dunked it in her soup, and ate it. A shadow darkened the table as Sir Kenton stopped behind where she sat.

"Lady Averella," the Shield said.

She clenched her hands beneath the table. Why would this man stand *behind* her? "I hear you, Sir Kenton, but I do not have eyes in the back of my head. If you wish to speak with me, do come around where I can see you."

For a moment, the beastly man did not budge, but then the shadow on the table shifted, and his imposing form came into view on her right.

"Lady Averella," he said again. "His Royal Highness wishes you to join him for dinner with your mother in Granton Castle."

Ah. Mystery revealed. Prince Gidon was annoyed that she had avoided him. He thought he could order her around. Well, he could not.

Averella ate her last bite of bread. She took her time to chew and swallow, then said, "As you can see, I have already eaten."

"That matters not." Sir Kenton grabbed her arm and jerked her off her bench.

Syrah gasped. Elzea cried out. And Averella did her best to keep her feet beneath her.

"Unhand me at—" Her command was cut short by Sir Kenton bending at the waist and throwing her over his shoulder. "Oh!"

The dining hall erupted with chatter as the adherents reacted to the breach in their normally tranquil domain. Syrah jumped to her feet and ran after Sir Kenton, who was already carrying the object of his quest out the door.

"Put me down at once!" Averella squirmed, kicked, and elbowed the back of Sir Kenton's head.

Whether from shock or fear, no one attempted to intervene. Sir Kenton carried her down the hall toward the foyer.

Averella tried again. "I said put me down!"

When he did not answer, she grabbed a fistful of his hair and pulled.

He did not even grunt.

Arman, help me! she prayed.

Sir Kenton was so much bigger and stronger than Averella that there was really nothing she could do to get away.

She took a deep breath and prayed, *Arman, keep me calm and levelheaded so I can think.*

He was taking her to her mother. For dinner. That was not so terrible, right?

Syrah remained behind them, and farther back, down the long hallway, Elzea followed with Father Sangee.

"You will regret this, Father!" Averella yelled. "My mother will see to that."

"I do beg your forgiveness, my lady," the priest called, "but I answer to my king before I answer to your mother."

His king... She wanted to yell out that he was not a king yet. How could any priest of Arman revere a man like Gidon Hadar? She simply could not comprehend it.

"I am sure you will love Sitna Manor," Averella yelled. "Because that is the only place you will be welcome..."

Sir Kenton shoved open the front door.

"...after your behavior to me." This she just managed to add before Sir Kenton ducked through the doorway and carried her out into the cold twilight.

6

The bailey bustled with the activity of vendors packing up their stalls for the day. Children chased each other, their laughter echoing off the stone curtain walls while a lone blacksmith pounded out a steady rhythm as he bent iron into a new shape. Along the bottom of the sentry wall, warming barrels held fires where some of the people congregated to rest and warm their hands.

Sir Kenton carried Averella through the throng, and the sight of her draped unceremoniously over his shoulder drew gasps and startled cries from those who recognized her. Syrah jogged behind them, hugging herself against the cold, breath fogging from lips quickly turning blue. Neither of them had been able to grab their cloaks and hats and gloves before Sir Kenton had committed his abduction.

"Syrah, find Captain Loam," Averella said. "Or any soldier."

"Yes, my lady." Syrah ran off through the bailey and out of Averella's sight. It was hard to see much of anything from this position. To make matters worse, Averella's hair had come loose from its pins and hung like a curtain over her face. She finally gathered it into her fist and held it beside her ear.

Whispers and murmurs spread like wildfire through the crowd. Faces turned, eyes widened in horror and disbelief.

"Lady Averella!" A peasant woman dropped her basket of fruit, sending apples rolling across the frosty dirt. "What is happening? Are you all right?"

"Sir Kenton is taking me inside," Averella said, elbowing the Shield in his lower back as hard as she could manage. "But I would much rather walk."

The peasant woman ran out of Averella's view. "Oh, sir," she said. "Might you put Lady Averella down so she can walk?"

"No," Sir Kenton said.

A guard, clad in chainmail with a sword at his side, ran up from the stables, his hand on his hilt. "Unhand her at once!" he commanded.

Sir Kenton spun around, and Averella put a hand on his lower back to steady herself.

"Take another step, and I'll snap her neck," he growled.

Averella's eyes bulged. "You most certainly will not!" she yelled. "Prince Gidon would never allow me to be hurt." Unless, of course, it was his idea...

She craned her neck to see and found those standing around them staring with a mixture of fear and helplessness in their eyes. Sir Kenton turned around and resumed his march toward the keep. There were three guards behind them now. The men exchanged anxious glances and followed at a distance, whispering among themselves.

"What do we do?" one said. "We can't just let him take her."

"We have no choice," another replied. "If we act, Lady Averella might be injured. We must wait for the right moment."

At this point, Averella found the whole ordeal mortifying. No one would ever forget the day Sir Kenton carried the heir to Carm Duchy across the bailey like a bushel of wheat. She wished she could do something to shame him, but struggling and beating him would only make her look weak.

"Thank you all for your care and concern," she called to those around her. "Sir Kenton is acting on Prince Gidon's orders to force me to see him after Mother and I refused. While their behavior is terribly rude, I do not believe they will harm me."

"Now see here, Sir Kenton. Put the lady down at once."

Finally! This was the voice of Captain Loam.

"I will do so only when I reach Duchess Amal's private dining room," Sir Kenton said.

"You would be wise to do so sooner," Captain Loam replied. "Your actions here today are an act of war."

War? Averella would not go that far, but it felt nice to have someone defend her honor.

"Take it up with your prince," was Sir Kenton's only reply.

"My lady?" Syrah reappeared, running around to Sir Kenton's back and jogging to keep up. "Are you well?"

At this point, to try and keep her head from being jostled by Sir Kenton's long strides, Averella had propped her elbow on the Shield's back and her cheek on the fist that still held her hair. "My head is tingling fiercely, and I am frightfully annoyed, but otherwise unharmed."

Yet Averella did not trust Prince Gidon not to try and force her to marry him. But how could she flee to Armonguard now? She had left her things in her room in the temple. She craned her neck to meet Syrah's gaze. "I will need my… belongings."

"Do not worry." Syrah lunged close and whispered, "I will pack you another bag."

Finally, Sir Kenton's boots traipsed up the front walk to the castle entrance. He carried her through the massive oak doors of the keep, where she saw Tristan Loam holding one of the double doors open. The captain of Carmine's army was as tall and broad as Sir Kenton but had hair the color of pumpkins and a belly that showed his love of pie.

Captain Loam released the door, the heavy thud echoing as it closed behind them. "Never you worry, my lady," he said, keeping pace with Syrah. "We will deal with this scoundrel momentarily."

Sir Kenton shook with rumbling laughter. "You will do no such thing, Captain."

Sir Kenton ascended the great staircase with determined strides, each step bringing them closer to Prince Gidon. Averella was so angry, she could not wait to tell the arrogant young prince exactly what she thought of his tactics.

They reached the hallway outside mother's private dining room. Hinges creaked as the door was opened and the odd processional trickled into the small space. The warm air was filled with the rich aroma of meats and fragrant herbs.

"Finally."

That, Averella knew, had been Prince Gidon's nasally voice.

After all the effort it had taken to avoid him, here they were. Well fine. There was nothing to do now but have it out, face to face.

But first Averella would make the wretched prince wait just a little longer. Sir Kenton set her on her feet. Her legs buckled momentarily, but she quickly found her footing. She took a moment to collect herself as her head still prickled from having been upside down for so long and her hands tingled as they began to thaw in the heat of the small room.

Syrah rushed to embrace her. "Oh, my lady! I'm so sorry."

The guards seized Sir Kenton and were about to wrestle him to the floor when an order from Mother stopped them.

"Release him, Captain Loam," Mother said. "I will have no more bloodshed this day."

Averella's stomach twisted as she met her mother's stoic expression. Bloodshed? Had someone been injured? Killed? Her gaze darted around the room, searching for any sign of violence or injury. The guards stood frozen, hands on their swords, ready to act but held back by Mother's order. Averella thought of her sisters and the servants dear to them. Who might have been harmed in this terrible ordeal?

Something pinched in Averella's temples, and she winced at the return of her tension headache. Just what she needed at such a precarious time.

Averella took that moment to determine who was seated around the table—which was laden with a feast already begun. Mother sat at one end, Prince Gidon at the other, and in the middle on mother's right, sat Lord Nathak, Prince Gidon's guardian, wearing his black leather half mask that hid the scarred portion of his face.

"A place has been set for you, Averella," Mother said, gesturing to the open seat. "Please join us. Captain Loam, you and your men are dismissed. Syrah, you may go as well."

While Captain Loam glared at Sir Kenton, he said, "Yes, Your Grace."

Averella clasped hands with Syrah, then her friend left the room with the soldiers.

"My dear lady Averella, you have kept me waiting for too long." Prince Gidon did not stand to greet her, but instead bit into a roasted turkey leg, which left flakes of parsley on his thin beard. The young man had a handsome face, almond brown skin, and oiled hair braided in a tail under a hammered brass circlet of ivy leaves. He wore a shirt of maroon silk with billowing sleeves that Gypsum would have loved.

"I did not know you were waiting for me, sir." Averella pulled out the chair across the table from Lord Nathak and sank onto the cushioned seat. "Master Talley said you were indisposed. Yet here you are, looking very well, indeed."

"I am much improved today." Gidon looked up, and his gaze combed over her head and torso as if looking for some flaw. "I do like that dress."

Ug. Averella had no stomach for complements from this lecherous serpent. A second throb in her temples made her wince. She reached for the goblet beside her plate and took a sip of wine. She should not be surprised that Gidon's presence in her home had rekindled her headache.

"Where is Father Sangee?" Lord Nathak asked.

Averella glanced up, surprised to see the man's visible eye fixed not on her but on Sir Kenton, who was standing along the wall behind the prince.

"I thought him right behind me," Sir Kenton said.

"Fetch him now!" Gidon cried.

Sir Kenton moved toward the door.

"Not you, Sir Kenton." Lord Nathak set his linen napkin on the table and stood. "I will find him. You must make sure Lady Averella stays in this room."

"Yes, sir," Sir Kenton said.

Averella glanced at her mother. "Are we prisoners, then? In our own home?"

"It appears so," Mother said.

The prince sighed. "I do not understand why this should be so tediously difficult. I want to marry. I should be able to marry."

"And marry you shall, Your Highness," Lord Nathak said. "I will return shortly."

Merciful heart. Did the prince expect to marry her now? Here? In the middle of a meal?

As Lord Nathak quitted the room, Averella looked again to her mother, who this time glanced at the four-panel folding screen in the corner of the room that not only blocked the sight of a sideboard—where servants could manage in private the overflow of food and drink from the table—but a secret door that led to Granton Castle's web of hidden passageways.

Yes, Averella had a way out if she needed one. Though to reach it, she would have to get past Gidon *and* Sir Kenton, who was standing very close to the screen. At the moment, she saw no way to do so. She was trapped.

7

"Who are you marrying, Your Highness?" Averella asked.

Gidon speared her with a glare that made her shrivel inside, but she fought to convey none of that fear on her face. "I grow bored of these games, my lady. You know full well I mean to marry you."

Averella took another sip of wine, hoping to quell her racing heart. "How odd. Did you not receive my answer from Master Talley?"

"Chora is a fool," the prince said. "He botched the whole thing."

"Did he?" Averella asked. "I find it strange that you would trust a mere servant with something so important. Unless, of course, you are afraid to speak for yourself."

Gidon pounded his fist on the table beside his trencher. "I am not afraid. And I have spoken of this repeatedly."

"Yet I have never once heard you ask me such a thing," Averella said.

His eyes narrowed. "If that will please you, fine. Lady Averella, will you marry me?"

She waited a moment, as if giving the matter a bit of thought, then said, "I am honored by the request, Your Highness, but no, thank you."

A flush rose above the dark beard line on Gidon's cheeks. "Why do you continually refuse your future king?"

"My daughter means no offense, sir," Mother said. "But she has already pledged her hand to another."

Thick eyebrows sank over those penetrating blue eyes. "What other?"

Averella would not put Bran's life in danger by revealing his identity to this ruthless young man. "That, sir, is not your business," she said.

The prince stood so quickly that his chair fell over behind him. "You dare speak so—"

The door opened, and Lord Nathak entered with Father Sangee.

"Forgive me, Your Highness," Father Sangee said, coming to stand at the corner of the table between Averella's and Gidon's seats. "I got lost in this monstrous castle, and no one would show me the way."

Averella had little doubt that her mother had bloodvoiced orders to Anillo to have the servants do that very thing should the traitorous priest enter the fortress.

"You retain the most insolent servants, Your Grace," the priest added.

"I'm sorry they displeased you, Father," Mother said.

Gidon flung his arm toward Averella like a petulant child tattling to an elder. "She refuses me still!"

"Never mind that," Lord Nathak said to Gidon, his tone soothing. Then he turned to the priest. "Father? Let's get this done, shall we?"

Heat flooded through Averella. The walls themselves seemed to close in on her as her heart slammed against her ribs, fighting to escape. "Do you honestly believe you will force me to marry you this moment?"

"I am your future king, and consequently your master." Gidon fixed her with a pointed stare as he loomed over her chair. "You *will* obey me."

Averella could not prevent her lip from curling if she had wanted to. "I see," she said. "Well, since you wish me to suffer and be unhappy for the rest of my life, I suppose I shall have to face it as best I can."

"That's the spirit, my lady," Father Sangee said. "Arman blesses the obedient."

That comment sent fire up Averella's spine. "Is that what you have been, Father? Obedient?"

"Why, yes, my lady," Father Sangee said.

Averella glanced at Lord Nathak. "What reward did you offer this man for his *obedience* today?"

"Reward?" Lord Nathak raised his eyebrows, all innocence, it seemed.

She turned her focus on Gidon. "Yes, reward."

"Father Sangee wishes to be pontiff of the Armanite faith," Gidon said. "He will move to Armonguard with us and serve there."

Averella met her mother's gaze and exchanged a look of under-standing. So *that* explained it.

"As I said, my lady. Arman blesses the obedient." Father Sangee clasped his hands together and glanced skyward in a silent prayer of thanksgiving.

The prince's expression softened, and he stepped toward Averella, who still sat in her chair. "I do not wish for you to live in misery, my dear," he said. "You shall want for nothing."

She scoffed. "Except my freedom."

The cold, calculating expression returned. "Precisely. I'm glad we finally understand each other."

Horrible man. The way to the passage in the corner was currently blocked. Averella's mind whirled as she sought another means of escape. "Will you at least let me change into a more appropriate gown?" she asked and pointedly looked down at the simple dress she had been wearing while working in the temple.

"That will not be necessary," Gidon said.

"What of my sisters?" Averella asked, glancing to her mother for some sort of vocal support. "Can I not have at least one stand up with me?"

Gidon glanced at Lord Nathak who shook his head.

"No." Gidon snapped his fingers at Father Sangee. "Begin, Father."

"Yes, of course." The priest cleared his throat. "You come here today of your own free will to—"

"Best skip that part, Father," Lord Nathak said, glancing first at Averella and then to her mother.

"Quite right," Father Sangee said. "Uhm, whose blessings accompany you? No, that won't do either, I suppose. Let's see... The betrothed should join hands."

Averella scooted her chair away from Gidon, clasping her hands in her lap as the prince reached for her.

"Father Sangee." Mother got up and made her way toward Averella and the priest. "You cannot perform a marriage blessing without the consent of both parties. What you are doing goes against the very tenants of our faith."

"How can I deny my future king?" the priest said. "I value my life more than that."

"You are wise, Father," Lord Nathak said. "Do not doubt that the duchess seeks to save her own neck, as well, or she would not have invited us to dine."

"Do you honestly believe that, Lord Nathak?" Mother asked. "You three are hopelessly outnumbered by my army. No, I am not afraid for my life but for the lives of my people, which you value so little."

"Stand up!" Gidon moved to pull Averella up by force.

She pushed back her chair and stood before he could touch her, not so much to comply but to be ready should Mother create enough of a distraction to open up a means of escape.

The prince reached for her hands. He wore a ring on every one of his fingers and thumbs. She drew back.

"Oh, for pity sake." He lunged forward and grabbed her hands, squeezing them until she nearly yelped in pain.

"Your Highness," Father Sangee said. "If it is your will to be bound to this lady, place a ring on her finger."

"What ring?" Prince Gidon glanced across the table to Lord Nathak.

"Give her one of yours," Lord Nathak said.

"All right." Gidon released her and splayed his fingers before him, frowning. She bit back a laugh that this vain man might struggle to decide which of his many jewels to part with.

Mother took that moment to push between Averella and the prince so that she was standing right before Father Sangee. "Does not the Book of Life urge us to obey Arman rather than men?"

"Yes, Your Grace," Father Sangee said, "but it also reminds us to be submissive and obedient to our rulers and authorities."

"I am not afraid of those who threaten to kill me," Mother said. "They cannot touch my soul, which belongs to Arman. To whom does your soul belong, Father?"

Father Sangee sputtered. "You dare question my faith?"

"Here!" Gidon pulled a ring from his pinky finger and thrust it out, but Averella had edged behind her mother and the priest.

"What is happening?" Gidon exclaimed, throwing up his hands. "Am I marrying the duchess now? Where is Lady Averella?"

"Sir Kenton," Lord Nathak said. "Please subdue Duchess Amal until this wedding is over."

"You wouldn't dare." Mother spun toward Lord Nathak, keeping herself between Averella and the others in the room. She motioned behind her back for Averella to flee.

"Your Grace, you leave us no choice," Lord Nathak said.

Gidon stepped back to allow Sir Kenton access to Mother, who inched back little by little, cleverly drawing the Shield down the side of the table.

Averella continued to shift the opposite way. She had a clear path now but for Father Sangee. She had hoped to slip quietly past him, but his girth removed stealth as an option. She currently stood right in front of the real exit, but she did not know who was waiting outside. She did open the door, however, letting it swing just a crack. Hopefully, once the confusion died down, everyone would think she slipped out that way.

Sir Kenton lunged toward Mother, and the moment her piercing scream drew everyone's attention, Averella rammed her shoulder into Father Sangee's lower back, shoving him into Gidon. Then she slipped behind the screen to her left and deftly slid the hidden pocket door panel into the wall. She spun into the dark passage and quickly glided the panel shut again.

Darkness closed around her. She remained perfectly still, not wanting to make any sound that might alert the men to her presence.

"Get off me, man!" Gidon's voice rose above the rest of the commotion on the other side of the hidden door. "Can you not stand on your own two feet?"

"She pushed me!" Father Sangee said, his voice almost as petulant as Gidon's had been before.

"Who pushed you?" Gidon asked.

"Lady Averella has left us," Lord Nathak said. "The door is open."

Prince Gidon screamed a foul curse word that brought a smile to Averella's lips. She pursed them tightly to keep from releasing the giggle that threatened to bubble up from her stomach.

"Find her, Kenton," Gidon said.

"I'm afraid not," Mother said. "Captain Loam?"

The sounds of dozens of hobnails on polished wood were so loud that Averella seized the moment to slip down the passageway to the peephole. She pressed her nose against the cold wood of the wall and looked into the dining room. She found it filled with the gold and maroon uniforms of Carmine. So many soldiers that she could not see her mother.

"Your Highness, Lord Nathak, Sir Kenton, and Father Sangee," Captain Loam barked. "Duchess Amal has asked us to escort you from the property."

The Carmine soldiers formed two lines, making a clear path straight for the door.

"You're kicking us out?" Lord Nathak asked.

"With as much niceties as we can muster after the way you have treated the Amal family," Captain Loam said.

"I demand you bring Lady Averella back here at once," Gidon said.

"I'm afraid I can't do that, Your Highness," Captain Loam said.

"Kenton, kill this man," Gidon said.

"I have been disarmed, Your Highness," Sir Kenton said.

"You hold no authority over me." Gidon swore again. "I am the future king."

Captain Loam merely gestured to the door. "Yet you are not king at the moment," he replied. "You were a guest here at the duchess' pleasure, but her pleasure is at an end."

"Let us depart from this place, Your Highness." Lord Nathak shrugged free of the grip of one of the guards. "We should rethink this plan to marry you to any woman as deceitful and rude as Lady Averella Amal."

Gidon's chest heaved as he breathed through his nose, his mouth pressed into a straight line. Suddenly, his rigid posture relaxed, and he smiled. "You are wise, Lord Nathak. I deserve a bride who will adore me as much as she will be loyal."

"That you do, Your Highness," Lord Nathak said.

"Besides, I don't need to marry to control this land." Prince Gidon walked slowly between the rows of Carmine soldiers, Sir Kenton on his heels. "Once I am crowned king, I shall revoke the dukedom title from the Amal family. They have proved most disloyal to Er'Rets."

Lord Nathak followed Sir Kenton out. "You are wise, Your Highness. We must have allegiance in the north."

Averella leaned back from the peephole and rolled her eyes. Prince Gidon would have a difficult time finding allegiance anywhere. King or not, he was too much of a bully.

"You as well, Father Sangee," Captain Loam's voice filtered through the wall. "You are to vacate at once."

"Surely her Grace doesn't mean for me to leave the temple," Father Sangee said.

Averella looked through the peephole again. The priest stood at the doorway with Captain Loam. All but three soldiers had left with the prince.

"You have been reassigned, Father," the captain said.

"She cannot reassign me!" Father Sangee said. "She is not the pontiff."

"No, but she has bloodvoiced Pontiff Fonshaw and gained his permission. He agreed with her complaint against you."

"What complaint?"

"On the grounds that you conspired against her after you signed your name as witness to her rejection of the prince's proposal."

"But he is to be our king!"

"The pontiff would like to see you in Armonguard as soon as you can reach him. Duchess Amal has graciously loaned you the use of a horse and wagon and a military escort to keep you safe on the long journey."

The priest stammered. "This is outrageous. I am needed at the Carmine temple. They will be lost without me."

"They will have to rely on Arman for support until your replacement arrives," Captain Loam said. "I daresay Arman is up to the task."

Father Sangee's complexion looked slightly green, but he finally stormed out of the dining room. The soldiers followed, leaving Captain Loam alone.

"The duchess will be in her office," he said to seemingly no one, then left, closing the door behind him.

Averella leaned against the wall in the dark corridor and shuddered. That had been too narrow of an escape for her liking. She had a nagging sense that they had not yet seen the end of the prince nor heard the last of his scheme to gain power through her family. At least no one had been hurt.

No, wait. Mother had said something about bloodshed. Averella must get the full story from her mother right away. She had to know who had been hurt and how they fared.

"**C**ale Gensen? Killed?" Averella sank into the chair opposite her mother's desk. Her mind whirled at the news, refusing to believe it. Cale was but a messenger, a young one at that, with an entire life ahead of him. "How? When?"

"Cale brought word back from Father Sangee that you refused to come to dinner," Mother said. "The prince was livid and ordered him to go back and drag you here. Cale said he could never do that, so the prince ordered Sir Kenton to kill him, then fetch you himself."

Averella pressed her hands against her face. Had she known Sir Kenton had just killed Cale when he was carrying her from the temple, she would have been more violent in her attempts to get free. "It is my fault."

"No, dearest. It's Prince Gidon's fault."

Averella wiped the tears from her cheeks. "Will he truly take Carm Duchy from you when he becomes king?"

"He might try." But the look in Mother's eyes said he would have quite a fight ahead of him if he did.

How many more could lose their lives like Cale should they choose to resist? Yet what life might they expect to have if they simply acquiesced to a tyrant's whims?

"A coronation is less than a year away," Averella said. "Is there nothing we can do?"

"Father Sangee is leaving," Mother said, "so that is a start. It is nearly impossible to know, however, if everyone working on this estate is loyal to me over the prince."

"It is a lot to ask, is it not?"

"It is. I myself don't like disobeying my future king, but it has not yet been officially decided that he will inherit over his uncle."

"Prince Oren would make a wonderful king," Averella said. "I planned to go there tonight. Run away and beg his help."

"Yes, Anillo said as much. Many agree with you about Prince Oren. The direct line of descent places Prince Gidon ahead of his uncle in the order of succession, but the Council of Seven still must vote on the matter once he comes of age. They could very well vote for Prince Oren instead."

"But not until next spring," Averella said.

"That's right."

"Do you think he'll take the advice of Lord Nathak? That he'll find another bride willing to accept his suit?"

"He will find plenty of women to worship him without needing to marry any of them," Mother said. "But he wants control of the north, and the only way to do that is to ally with Carm Duchy. I fear for you now more than ever. He will wait until we grow lax, then make his move."

"You do not think he will try to reassign the duchy, like he said?"

Mother smiled grimly. "Lord Nathak knows me well enough to recognize that I would not allow just anyone to take over this land, even if my sovereign decreed it. They will do all they can to avoid war with me. Right now, they have no army to speak of. Five hundred soldiers in Sitna, at best, and I'm being generous. The majority of the army in Armonguard is loyal to Prince Oren, though some of them might go north should the prince call for reinforcements. Lord Nathak has done the prince a disservice, keeping him in Sitna all these years. Had he raised Gidon in Armonguard, the army would know him."

"And hate him as much as I do."

"Some certainly would. But men tend to obey rank more than they rely on emotions. They would do their duty."

"And what will you do?" Averella could not imagine losing her home to someone loyal to Prince Gidon.

"I will serve as a member of the Council of Seven and make Prince Gidon's unacceptable behavior known. I will keep in close contact with Prince Oren. I will continue to build my own army and defenses. And I will keep you away from *both* Prince Gidon and Lord Nathak. Marriage is still their best plan to take this duchy without a war."

"Then I will follow through with my plan to leave," Averella said. "Pretend to go to Tsaftown, but go to Armonguard instead. Do you think Prince Oren will shelter me?"

"I am sure he would, dearest, and that is why Armonguard is not the best plan."

Heat coiled within Averella's chest. "Why not?"

"Because Prince Oren could not keep your visit a secret. Word would get out and eventually reach Gidon. He would see Prince Oren choosing to help you as an act of war. And if that were not trouble enough, we don't want to give anyone reason to think Prince Oren is actively trying to keep the throne from his nephew. Oren must be blameless so that the Council might be able to compare the two and see Gidon for what he is."

Averella could not refute her mother's wisdom. "But where else can I go?"

"I have thought a lot about this," Mother said. "You are wise to make it look as if you have gone to Tsaftown. Instead, you must go to Walden's Watch and stay with Coraline."

That tiny place? "But, Mother. If my presence would be discovered in Armonguard, it will happen even faster in Walden's Watch. That place is so small, I promise you, before the day ends, the entire community will know I am there."

Mother frowned. "Perhaps if you used a different name..."

Averella wrung her hands and fingered the nail she had chipped today as she scrubbed pews. She looked up. "I could go in disguise. As a servant."

"A servant! Averella, no. Despite my best efforts, I cannot even assure the safety of the serving girls in my own household. Coraline would have to conceive of a way to protect you. It would be too dangerous otherwise."

"Surely she could find a way," Averella said.

Mother tipped her head to one side, brows pinched. Then she lit up, and a slow smile turned her lips.

"What?" Averella asked. "You have an idea. Tell me!"

"You will only be safe if you pretend to be a boy."

Averella sat on the chaise lounge, trying to take this in. "You think I would make a convincing boy?"

"A stray boy. With an orange tunic, trousers, and no face powder, no one will doubt it."

Averella brushed her palm down the front of her dress. "You seem to have forgotten my insecurities about my looks."

Mother sank beside Averella and took hold of her hands. "Dearest, I mean no insult by this scheme. Any of us could look the part of the opposite sex with a little effort."

"I daresay *you* could not."

"Oh, pish posh. This is not a time to pout. Prince Gidon has but a handful of months until he must marry—at the very least announce his betrothal. That's not so long to hide away, is it?"

Averella fingered her chipped nail. "I suppose not."

"Now, before we send you off, I have one more thing to discuss. These past few days and earlier, in the dining room, I have tried to speak to your mind. Did you not hear me?"

Averella thought about it. "No. Should I have? I was shielded, like you said."

"I had still hoped you might hear me." Mother twisted her lips. "It often feels like a pinch to your head, almost at your temples. Then you usually hear a voice announcing the intent to speak."

Averella's lips parted slightly. The headaches. Suddenly, they all made sense. Mother had been trying to bloodvoice her. "I thought they were headaches," she said. "But I never once heard your voice."

"That is uncommon but not unheard of for a beginner." Mother sighed. "You are very good at shielding. A little too good, it seems."

Averella did not like that her bloodvoicing gift already might be broken before she had even started to use it. "Should I not shield then?"

"No, no. You must keep your mind hidden at all times. As I said before, Lord Nathak can bloodvoice, and he has friends who can as well. They will be looking for you. For your mind."

"Cannot bloodvoicers hide their minds?" Averella asked.

"Yes, but there is no time to train you, my dearest," Mother said. "And it will not be safe for us to practice with you so far away. While it would have been nice for us to be able to bloodvoice each other, we will have to make do. Keep your shields just as firm as you have been. That will be safest."

"I suppose I cannot pack for this trip?" Averella asked.

"Is there something you want to take with you?"

"My Book of Arman?"

"No, a stray should not own a book like that. It's far too expensive."

Gypsum would have begged to take her embroidery kit or paints, but Averella rather liked the fact that she would not be expected to be artistic for a few months.

"I guess there is nothing else I would want. Not really. As long as someone waters my plants."

"I will ask Anillo to do so."

"Can I say farewell to Syrah and my sisters?" Averella asked.

Mother twisted her lips and gazed at Averella. "I think not. Had you run away from the temple tonight as you had originally planned, you would not have seen them. Better that they are kept in the dark about where you truly are. Safer for everyone."

Averella saw the wisdom there. "Very well."

"Now, wait here while I speak with Coraline and Anillo. Do not leave this room. Is that clear?"

Averella sighed, feeling trapped yet again but relieved to finally have a plan. "Yes, Mother."

Mother returned, arms laden with clothing and supplies. First, she cut Averella's hair. Poorly. On purpose.

"A stray would have to cut his own hair," she explained.

Mother also refused to let Averella use her front-lace stays.

"They give too much shape to your waist," was her reasoning.

Instead, Mother wrapped Averella in a long strip of linen to hide what very little shape she had in her chest.

"This is worse than the stays," Averella said. "I can barely breathe!"

Mother's only response was, "Make do."

"What if I need to change?"

"Coraline will help. She is very excited about your visit and has already found you a place to apprentice that will keep you out of the manor house and harm's way. I thought it might be odd for a stray to serve as an apprentice, but Coraline assures me that it will be acceptable in Walden's Watch."

A job? "What kind of apprenticeship?"

"At an apothecary." Mother quirked her eyebrows. "Are you pleased?"

Averella fought a smile. "I suppose that would be diverting."

"I thought you'd like it. Prince Gidon can search Er'Rets high and low for you, but he will not be looking for a stray boy healer."

"I am certain you are right about that," Averella said dryly.

Then came the tunics. Seven, in all, making Averella feel like she had gone hunting with her Uncle Edik, all bundled up for an ice storm.

"Why so many?" Averella asked.

"A plump boy will not be pressured into military service. With your figure and your apprenticeship at the apothecary, you should be left well enough alone."

Averella flubbed her lips. "I feel as though I am going into battle. I cannot imagine even the sharpest sword could piece through so many layers."

"I am sorry you're uncomfortable," Mother said. "While it is not as cold there as it is here, it will be chilly so near the sea. I doubt very much you will mind the warmth then."

Averella supposed that once she was away on her own, she could choose how many layers to wear and how many to leave behind.

"Tomorrow, I will send Anillo to the temple to gather the things you left behind," Mother said. "He will make a scene about discovering your packed bag and the letters you wrote. In response, we will send a squadron to Tsaftown to try and track you down."

"Those poor soldiers," Averella said. "Having to travel north this time of the year."

"Do not worry about them. Now, Anillo has gathered a few more things." Mother motioned to a stack of fabric on one of the chairs before her desk. "You have two extra pairs of trousers, plus a small sack filled with the makings of a healer's kit."

Averella picked up the leather satchel from the pile and peeked inside. There were a few small empty jars and several sprigs of herbs wrapped separately in linen. She sighed. "Will you tell Bran where I have gone? When he returns?"

"Only if I deem it safe to do so," Mother said. "Though I do promise to tell him *why* you've gone so he will not worry."

Averella's heart ached. "He will worry no matter what, but he will understand."

"It's settled then. The next time our dear prince inquires after your presence, I will have no choice but to tell him you've run away."

"In my absence, will not Lord Nathak continue to press his suit with you?"

"Let him try," Mother said. "I rather enjoy rejecting that man."

Averella scratched at the coarse weave of the stray tunic. "I am not sure I will ever get used to a boy's costume."

"Come." Mother waved her to the mirrorglass on the wall to the right of her desk. See how you look."

Averella crossed the room and gasped at who she saw looking back from the reflection. "I look fat... and like a stray boy."

"Good. Let's say you're fourteen. That will better fit your height and small frame."

Averella supposed that made sense. She wrinkled her nose. "Who decided strays must wear this ghastly shade of orange?"

"It is a rather dreadful color, is it not?"

Averella smoothed down the short hair over her eyes. "Did you have to give me bangs?"

"Boys wear bangs," Mother said.

"Do they? I cannot think of one boy I have ever seen with hair like this."

"I did my best."

Averella glanced at her mother, whose eyes shone with unshed tears. "Oh, Mother, do not cry." She embraced her, which made the woman break down.

"I'm sorry it's come to this, dearest," Mother said. "Promise me you'll take care."

"I promise."

Mother squeezed her once more, then pulled away. "Anillo will be waiting in the cellar. You're to join a group of men taking an order of wine to the coast. You'll board a ship there and sail straight to Walden's Watch. Coraline promised she would be waiting for you at the dock."

Averella knew this already. Mother had gone over it nearly a dozen times. "I will be fine."

"Remember not to be so well-spoken. You'll stand out like a lily in a field of dandelions. And you're Vrell Sparrow now, don't forget. Not Averella."

"Vrell Sparrow." Averella tried out the name as she took one last look at herself in the mirrorglass. "I suppose it will have to do."

NOT THE END

This story continues in the novel *By Darkness Hid*.

About the Author

J ill Williamson is a multi-passionate creative who loves the arts. She has written over thirty books for readers of all ages. Her debut novel, the medieval fantasy adventure *By Darkness Hid*, won an EPIC Award, a Christy Award, and was named a Best Science Fiction, Fantasy, and Horror novel of 2009 by VOYA magazine. She considers herself a "storyworld first" novelist, as she starts new projects by first building the world, then characters and plot. Jill loves working with other writers and encouraging them to respect their dreams. She speaks and gives writing workshops at libraries, schools, camps, and conferences. She is most recently a producer of films, working closely with her writer/director husband and other creatives in the Pacific Northwest.

To be notified of new releases and to get a free short story (ebook or audio), visit jillwilliamson.com/sanctumand subscribe to her email newsletter. You can support Jill and her writing on her Patreon page at patreon.com/JillWilliamson. You can also find Jill on the following social media platforms:

9 781955 843997